Adventures
Of Bumper

The Bali Bunny

By

Linda Higgins

Adventures of Bumper

Please note the author occasionally uses Indonesian or
Balinese words.

ISBN: (E-book)

ISBN: 9781941125557 (Paperback)

Library of Congress Control Number:

Website: www.lindahiggins-author.com

Table of Contents

BUMPER

Hi, my name is Bumper, as given to me by my very best friend, whom I will introduce you to later. But first I want to give you some insight as to how we met. I am not sure exactly which village I was born in, since at about one month old I was orphaned and moved to a very small and crowded home.

At first there were ten of us in our space with just enough room to turn around, but as my brothers and sisters began to be selected, I was able to stretch my legs a little and was very fortunate to receive a larger share of food. I guess that way of looking at the separation kept me from getting sad. This extra space and food only lasted for a week when the head master decided to move some strangers in with us. Let me tell you, they were a different breed of character, small furry pigs, all with the same name, Guinea. I tried to count how many there were but they were always moving around and I lost my numbers. We got along OK, they left me alone and visa-versa. I think the greatest annoyance was all the dogs in the pens next to ours. What made them think they could bark all day and all night long? In addition to that, the greatest hardship was the fact that I could not fluff my fur. I kept as clean as possible, for my tongue is small, pink, and soft as velvet. Not suitable for tugging at the straw that was matted in my long silky fur. I would lick my toes on the front paws, and sitting upright, try to at least groom my huge ears. I believe it was about 4 months, and just my cousin and I were left, a real bully since he had grown much faster than I and that meant he got to eat first and what was left was for me.

I remember this smiling man came by and looked at me, talking real quiet with the head master. They said something about not being baby bunnies and the smiling man referred to us as big. Yes, my jumbo cousin was, but not me. Then he walked away, I really wanted to get out of here and thought just maybe this could be my lucky day, but they walked away and left us behind. I then heard the footsteps of the smiling man as he returned, and now he was capable for he was carrying a box. This smiling man pointed at me saying "that's the one for us. Hello my name is Thomas." The next thing I knew it was into a carry box and away we went, to where, I had no idea. I was really scared because it was so dark in the box at first, then my eyes began to glow, there was nothing to see, it was still dark, but everything smelled so much cleaner and fresher. I could not hear any more dogs barking so I shook off my fear and was able to relax. After a long ride the truck came to stop and I heard talking, then the box was lifted up and carried a short distance. Again voices and this time I heard a new voice, much softer and very kind. As the top of the box was pried open, our eyes meet for the first time, this beautiful lady looked at me and let out the loudest scream I had ever heard. Scared me nearly to death. Then, with this gentle smile she bent over and picked me up, holding me so close to her, and such a wonderful fragrance she had. Her first words, which were after the scream, were "how fluffy you will be after a nice brushing." From that moment I was in love with Laura, my best friend.

My life had changed for the better. I had the freedom to run, hop and sleep as much as I wanted, but always watched over by Laura. This allowed me the ability to practice my quick starts and turns. Laura noticed that the bright sun hurt my eyes and she told me she had an idea to design hats to help shade my eyes. To me that sounded kind of silly, never heard of a rabbit with a hat. But Laura explained to me that it served two purposes. First, to protect my eyes, and second, as a medal like a hero gets for being special. Since I don't have a uniform to pin it on, a hat would be the same thing, but for bunnies. I would be the first decorated bunny in the world, and well deserved for doing my very best. So let me share with you some of my adventures that earned my decorations. Then I will share with you some adventures that Laura did not know about.

VERANDAH HAT

Papaya is so delicious on a hot evening, cut into cubes and chilled. Bumper will have it for desert and sometimes eats three pieces in one setting. One of his best friends grows papaya. He has many trees and never fails to share the harvest. Riding a motorcycle to their house with a gift of fruit, his name is Jawana. On this particular weekend he is going to take care of Bumper while Laura and Thomas go to Singapore. Jawana is very polite, with perfect manners. He has been working very hard putting in extra hours on the job, since his recent promotion to night manager at the Beach Front Hotel in Bali. Looking forward to relaxing for a few days with Bumper, he has planned for them to watch TV, with snacks of swizzle sticks and peanuts. Jawana arrived right on time.

With treats in hand, they settled down to enjoy the evening television program, a magician who had rabbits that could hide so well everyone thought they disappeared in the hat. Bumper said "rabbits are very clever at hiding," but Jawana insisted it was magic.

It was one hour into the show when the phone rang. Jawana answered the phone, "Good evening. Yes sir, this is Jawana. I am staying with a friend who is under my care. Yes, thank-you, of course sir, I will bring him along. Thank-you sir, we will leave right away." Ayo (let's go) Bumper, put on your hat, we are going to the Beach Front Hotel."

"Oh fabulous," Bumper replied, "I'm going to wear my evening verandah hat. It was presented to me for good manners and I usually wear it when Laura and Thomas have tea, and we all sit at the small table. I get milk with just a sprinkle of sugar and cinnamon. She always says how elegant I look with my little purple feathered hat that sparkles under the stars. Also Jawana, don't forget my toss, the large bamboo basket that I always travel in."

The toss was strapped onto the motorcycle and they were off. Upon arrival they headed straight to the head office to meet the boss.

"Hello Jawana, where is your friend?" The boss asked.

"Here, in his toss, may I introduce you to Bumper." Jawana replied.

"What a delightful pleasure to meet you, Mr. Bumper," the boss said. "Sorry to have to inconvenience your evening. However, we have a guest who has received a most urgent fax and must leave for home immediately. There are documents to be endorsed prior to his departure and will require a brief meeting. Perhaps Mr. Bumper would like a piece of carrot cake while he waits. We will go to the suite and have room service."

In the suite Jawana placed Bumper on the lush carpet. He then carried the toss into the bedroom, where he saw a neat stack of luggage near the door and this is where he placed the toss. Bumper followed him, and seeing the huge King size bed, jumped as high as he could, landing softly onto it. Removed his hat and laid stretched out with his back legs behind him as far as they could reach, and did the same with his front.

"Bumper, this should not take too much time, I will come back for you soon," said Jawana.

"Oh, take your time, I am enjoying all this luxury, very, very comfortable."

Jawana left just as the snack arrived. The waiter opened the double French doors that led to the verandah, where he placed the cake and milk on a table for two. As the waiter left, he stared at the little furry guest stretched out on the bed and said, "Mr. Bumper, your desert is served."

Bumper left his hat where he had been resting and hopped off the bed, across the plush carpet, out the double doors and up onto the chair. He pointed his wiggle nose to heaven and said a prayer of thanks for the beautiful piece of cake that had a carrot cut to look like a rose on top of the thick white frosting, and a special thanks for Jawana who was always too much fun.

Bumper noticed how hot the night air was with few stars. *It's going to rain*, he thought. *It's going to rain in the near future as it usually does in Bali when the night is this intensely humid.* He began to eat his cake, determined to eat the whole big piece.

He was down to the last three bites when he heard Jawana call, "Bumper, where are you?" Bumper was feeling a little silly from all the sugar, and answered "I'm in the hat," then started to giggle. Jawana, who believed in magic, picked the hat up from the bed and left the room. Bumper, heard the door shut, hopped off the chair and bounced across the room as fast as he could saying, "I was only joking, wait, it was a joke." But it was too late, the room was silent and Jawana was gone. Bumper sat in the middle of the floor in front of the door. He tilted his head from side to side listening with one ear then the other but heard nothing. He listened with both ears wide and still nothing. Then he noticed his toss nearby, and thought, *surely Jawana will remember to come back for my toss*. It was past Bumper's bedtime so he hopped inside the toss to wait and fell fast asleep.

A porter entered the room to remove the luggage for the man who had the emergency, seeing the toss, this the porter also put on the baggage trolley. Taken to the waiting limousine, the suitcases put in the trunk, Bumper, asleep in his toss, was placed in the front seat with the driver. They went swiftly to the airport where a private jet was ready for takeoff. Baggage was placed in the cargo bay. The driver carried the toss to the stewardess and said "This is fragile, handle with care."

The stewardess, seeing the little bunny sound asleep inside the toss, smiled and said "Isn't he cute." She strapped the toss facing the window, to a seat on the airplane.

The plane flew all night. When Bumper woke he raised his head and out the window he saw an enormous rainbow. His eyes widened to get a better look. Colors were bright and so close he knew he could touch it as the plane flew through the rainbow to the other side.

Bumper heard someone say "What's this?"

The stewardess replied "Sir, it's your bunny."

"It's my what?" said a man's voice.

At that response, Bumper looked at the man and suddenly felt very timid. The man, realizing he may have frightened the little creature, sat down beside him.

"Well little fellow, where did you come from?" The man asked.

"I came from the Beach Front Hotel, my friend Jawana works there. Could we please phone him so he knows I'm all right and will be home soon? He is going to become so worried when I don't answer him from the hat."

"From the hat you say," and the man began to laugh. "Yes little fellow, we will phone immediately, not from the hat but from the jet." The man instructed the stewardess to inform Jawana that his friend was alright.

"But as to going home soon, that did present a problem. For you see, I have children and must not delay my return. Would it be possible for you to spend the week-end in my palace? This would give us time to plan your return," the man explained.

Bumper noticed this man possessed authority and dignity, qualities he admired. "By the way sir, my name is Bumper."

The man chuckled, answering "Pleased to meet you Mr. Bumper, I am the Sultan of Brunei." The Sultan then requested the stewardess to bring Bumper peanuts and broccoli. He loved broccoli, and ate seconds.

After landing, all was put in the limousine as before, except this time Bumper rode in the backseat with the Sultan. They drove through large gates, up a winding road and sure enough there it was - a palace.

"Your gardens look delicious," said Bumper, "but there is too much lawn in between the flowers, it's a very long way to go for a snack."

"We don't have any rabbits in our yard that snack, no rabbits at all," replied the Sultan.

"Not just for rabbits, there are butterflies, bumble bees, dragonflies, and birds to think of, and maybe squirrels, chipmunks and frogs." Bumper said.

"I had never thought of it that way, you're right, we need flower beds in the middle of the lawn and throughout," the Sultan agreed.

"Also around your palace and down the driveway. Daisies, and zinnias would be ideal. Zinnia is my favorite," advised Bumper.

"You're a very clever little bunny," stated the Sultan.

14

"You mentioned your children, do they play in the gardens?" asked Bumper.

"Sometimes their nanny will take them into the garden. My son and daughter are both still young. They are waiting for me and being young they cannot wait to long." explained the Sultan.

"Oh yes, children need to be seen and heard often. Seeing and hearing are my specialties," Bumper said.

"I am sure a visit with you would bring them a great amount of pleasure," replied the Sultan.

Entering the palace they were greeted by the servants, the Sultan walked with a graceful ease across the marble floors, which to Bumper were slippery. They came to a gigantic staircase. "Come along Bumper, we shall go directly to the children's playroom." The Sultan began to ascend the stairs. Bumper sat at the second step looking up. The Sultan smiled and said "Come on little fellow, I will give you a lift." He picked Bumper up, cuddling the soft fluffy fur.

The room they entered was huge. The sunlight streamed in through numerous big windows and the Sultan put Bumper on the floor. Bumper could not see and every time he took a hop he would bump into a toy, and there were a lot of exotic toys. A large ball of twine as big as a bush, and an ornate rocking camel with golden rope reigns and tassels. He could hear the giggles from the children and the cheerful greetings to their father the Sultan. Each child had been sitting in a small chair at a little table, one had been reading, the other drawing. Music drifted through the room, the softest sound of a harp, played by an attendant. Bumper just had to hop closer to the exquisite tones and bumped into the harp, causing the harpist to skip a note. This surprised the Sultan so he picked Bumper up and said "Children this is our new friend, appropriately named Bumper." The Sultan's children were delighted.

"Let him play here with us," requested the children.

"He has had a long journey and needs to rest," instructed the Sultan. So Bumper was placed on a satin pillow as big as a bed. Now, Bumper liked to sleep on his back, feet in the air, and that is just what he did. The children laid down to rest with him and they both fell fast asleep. When the children woke up it was dark. Seeing Bumper lay beside them with his eyes open and bright pink glow was exciting. Bumper can see clearly in the dark.

"Oh Bumper, I wish I could see in the dark," said the little boy.

"To see in the dark you would need to have big long ears. Would you want big long ears?" Bumper asked.

"Yes," answered the little boy. "That sounds wonderful to me."

"Consider, you could not see in the daylight and you would always have the long ears for better hearing. How would that make you feel?" Bumper asked the girl.

"I'm not sure which would feel better," the girl replied. "What do you think Bumper?"

"It's better to feel good about what you have, than to feel bad about what you don't have," Bumper answered.

"We could do that, where do we start?"

"By dreaming, when I want to dream I start by thinking of a happy place. This is what you do, make something up and describe it to me," advised Bumper.

"OK, I see a sky blue house with a red floor that sparkles, a bright yellow roof and windows that twinkle like stars. There's a yard with humble flowers like orange marigolds, white daisies and green leafy coleus," said the girl.

Astonished, Bumper stood upright on his hind legs and exclaimed "That sounds like my house! Your dream is true. If you could come with me for a visit and see for yourself."

"Where do you live?" the girl asked.

"I live on the other side of the rainbow." Bumper said.

In the morning the children woke full of energy and began to pack some clothes. When the nanny came in she was shocked to find their luggage in a neat stack ready to go.

"Where are you going?"

"Glorious day nanny, we have prepared for a short vacation," said the boy.

"We are going with Bumper to the other side of the rainbow for a visit," said the girl.

The family, so very grateful for the joy, decided to all go and make a holiday. The next day Bumper was home with his new friends, wearing the sparkly hat and sitting next to his Laura on his own Verandah having tea.

The children had found a dream, both the children and Bumper were wearing smiles.

VICTORY HAT

Strength, determination and ability to cooperate were factors in this remarkable story. The following is a factual account of the events of December 7, 1996.

Our home in Uma Alas, which is Balinese for Jungle/Rice Fields West, is situated near the river and far enough outside the main villages that electricity is undependable. To be sure that water is always available a large tower was built near the well to allow gravity rather than an electric pump to supply this necessity of life. Under the water tower is a brick foundation with the center full of rich black soil, just perfect for growing vegetables.

As usual Bumper was under strict supervision as he and Laura walked to the side of the house where Bumper likes to have his lunch under the water tower. Laura sat on the cement foundation as Bumper trimmed the vegetables. About two feet from where

Laura was, sitting wrapped around the branch of a bougainvillea, coiled and ready to strike was the deadliest snake on the island, the Ular Hijau (Green Snake). As Bumper moved in-between the snake and Laura, he turned his head as though he sensed danger but it was too late. The snake sprang forward as Bumper tried to move back but the poison fangs struck Bumper on his upper lip.

Laura realized quickly what had happened, grabbing Bumper and running to the house to summon help as the threads to his lifeline were shortened every second. Thomas, clear thinking and capable, took control of the situation as Bumper lay calmly in Laura's arms. With a bamboo stick Thomas cautiously approached the area of the attack, the snake had moved down the branch and into the grass. As the bamboo stick touched the bougainvillea, the snake raised his head and with a fast and direct hit the Ular Hijau was dead. Running back to the house, Thomas took the phone book and looked for a veterinarian as close to our home as possible, with the hope that they may have anti-venom. This should have been an unnecessary task, for nearly all humans who are bitten die. Thomas succeeded in finding the correct veterinarian, but without transportation their situation worsened. Gus, the yard boy, was given the phone to get the address and location. We had the address, Gus had written down but did not know the way. Our neighbor Mr. Sloan was home, and as fate would have it a friend was visiting him and knew exactly where this location was. We all jumped into Mr. Sloan's car and headed there directly.

Bumper was wrapped in a blanket, he lay limp in Laura's arms, and his face had swollen and was turning black around the bite area. As the Balinese friend noticed the swelling he knew of another veterinarian along the way and felt we had better stop and see if he has the necessary anti-venom. Time was critical for Bumper's survival.

We stopped along the road, and across the cow pasture was the home of another veterinarian. As we approached the house, three dogs began barking. It must have been terrifying for Bumper, however, he remained calm.

This veterinarian was not at home and we were directed to his office about one kilometer down the road. Back across the pasture, trying to walk quickly in flip-flops through thick mud. Arriving at the office, bursting in with urgency, the veterinarian weighed Bumper - 3 kilo, took his temperature - 90.5. Stating he did not have the serum, but offered to come with us and knew a shortcut to our original destination.

Back into the car, Bumper's face continuing to swell and discolor. The veterinarian was checking his watch again, telling Mr. Sloan cepht - cepht (quickly - quickly). Turning to us he said that since Bumper was bitten in the face, time was of the greatest essence. His chances were fading fast.

The shortcut took us through back roads and alleys. The rains had filled the potholes with water and turned the dirt into a thick mud. Inside the car not a word was spoken. It must have been that all were in prayer. Thomas later told Laura that he prayed, asking God not to take Bumper away from Laura. They need each other.

It had been 45 minutes when we arrived at the clinic. Bumper was ushered into a sick bay and placed on a tall table. Laying on his side, on top of his pink blanket, temperature taken again. The two veterinarians talked briefly. Stethoscope placed on his chest - heartbeat is strong. Anti-venom prepared, followed by two injections. The veterinarian told us that Bumper was very healthy and strong but you must understand that the venom is the most deadly in Bali. You will know the outcome in one hour, and I'm very sorry but I can't give you much encouragement. The time was 14:45 and we arrived home at 15:10.

We gave our thanks to all eight people who had urgently supplied help. Taking Bumper into the bedroom, we closed the doors, turned off the lights, pulled the curtains, turned on the fan and switched off the telephone. Laura sat down in a chair with Bumper on her lap. Lying on his back, his feet limp.

As 15:45 approached so did anxiety. Thomas sat on the floor next to Laura, rubbing Bumper's head. His face greatly out of proportion, black and purple near the bite area.

A sigh of relief and a momentary belief that our prayers had been answered at 15:50. Then the severity struck. Bumper had his first tremor. A sudden jerk of the body, we thought it was a heart attack. Then a calm, and breathing returned to normal. Seven minutes later it happened again just as before, then again about seven minutes later only with increasing pain. We got our stop watch to check the time between tremors.

They continued every seven minutes for an hour and a half. Bumper was becoming exhausted. Again it struck, only this time his breathing stopped. We called his name and gave him a slight shake, breathing resumed. Now totally exhausted and too tired to breath we gave him another shake, calling his name and petting his head to stimulate awareness. He must not pass-out.

At 17:45 he opened his eyes and his look was sweet when he recognized Laura and Thomas and knew we were all together helping. He gained some strength but the tremors continued, still seven minutes apart but with lessening of pain. By 18:30 he had passed the seven minute mark without a tremor. Then like a miracle at 18:45 he rolled over to lay on his tummy. Still very weak, but very much alive. He had a remarkable recovery and was given a green feathered hat for his "Victory."

Late that night there was the wildest storm we had ever seen. The sky was illuminated by lightning with applauding thunder. Bumper didn't seem the slightest bit afraid, as though he knew the heavens were in celebration of his victory. His guardian angel had been with him and went back to heaven to pronounce his success. So with joy, all angels were clapping, using lightning bolt as fireworks to glorify God and the power of his protection.

A thank-you note was sent to neighbor Sloan on Sunday 15-December-1996

Dear Mr. Sloan,

Thank you for helping God save my life.

In a time when every second was measured you did not hesitate.

Your effort provided the opportunity for a miracle.

May God bless you,

I hope to follow your example.

Believe me to be

Very Sincerely

–BUMPER

CHRISTMAS HAT

It was December, Bumper had been looking forward to Christmas day. One week earlier, Blitzen the reindeer came to his house with Santa, a very kind gentleman Bumper immediately liked. Laura was thrilled and Santa asked if we had seen Rudolph. Santa had lost his red nosed reindeer. He seemed forlorn about the prospects of delivering gifts without his special lead deer.

"Bumper," Santa said, "you wonderful little bunny, you could help. Would you?"

"Oh yes, please allow me. What may I accomplish?" Bumper asked."

"We need your guidance in the dark," Santa stated.

"I can see clearly and brightly. You need not worry nor fear the way, for I have a guardian angel," replied Bumper.

That afternoon Bumper's lunch of cabbage and carrots were packed. Santa helped him aboard the sleigh, saying "Ho Ho Ho away we go," and, they were off. Waving goodbye to Laura, the sleigh headed for the North Pole. Climbing higher and higher, it became darker and colder. Passing many stars, Bumper saw one that was not a star at all. Alerting Santa who saw nothing, Bumper not only saw the mysterious glow that was different to him in many ways from normal stars, he also heard with his precious ears, a sort of humming. Now he began pleading with Santa to make a detour and investigate.

Santa admired Bumper's audacity and respected his talents, but Santa had a tight delivery schedule and a very long way yet to go. Oh, what to do? Then he remembered, it was Christmas time and not a time to flounder over decisions. Bumper was clever and he did possess the rabbit's foot good luck charm. God Bless him, why not? Where to go Bumper - lead the way.

They disappeared so high in the sky Santa was dazzled by passing stars, and saw nothing but the same in the far distance. Bumper stood on his back legs, his head above Blitzen's for a better view. He took hold of the reins and ever so gently guided the loyal reindeer. Bumpers eyes were aglow and ears were pitched forward. This way then that way. It was getting colder. His fur rippled in the wind and then he came upon a midnight clear. Bumper began hopping up and down.

"Over there," Bumper pronounced.
"Where?" Santa asked.
"Over there – see?"
"Yes! Thank you my angle of mercy."

"It's Rudolph and his antler is frozen to that star." Bumper hopped to the reindeer and with his

31

warm fur, melted the antler free. With Rudolph's extraordinary speed they gained time and delivered Bumper home with heartfelt gratitude, to enjoy Christmas with his Laura, her dearest Thomas, and many friends and neighbors. Bumper enjoyed Christmas wearing a new special made hat and shook paws with all the guest, many of whom asked "Bumper sweetie, what have you been doing?"

"Trying to be good," he said in his timid way.

And that you are my precious one. Merry Christmas and God Bless You.

THE HAMMOCK HAT

Regardless of weather, Bumper receives a brushing every day. He is very particular about keeping clean and fluffy. After the brushing he is wrapped in a big towel and then he always sleeps. Daytime is for napping. He has special vision in the dark, so likes to rest his eyes when the sun is out. May as well, he can't see a thing in the bright afternoon light. Usually he gets to swing in the hammock on the front porch with the warm sea breeze tickling his ears. To shade his eyes, Bumper wears an adorable pink and white ruffled crochet hat with a large pink satin ribbon. The top of the hat is open to allow for his big ears.

On this particular day, Mr. Don was visiting Bali and his closet friends Laura and Thomas. He had raised rabbits and knew all about them. But he had never met a rabbit like Bumper.

One of the activities that Mr. Don planned for his vacation, was to take photographs of the international surfing competition. He had brought with him a good camera. Just as he was bringing his gear to the porch, getting ready to go down to the beach, he noticed Bumper in the hammock sound asleep. He had to get a picture or no one would believe it. Putting down his towel and beach gear he snapped a couple of photographs. The phone rang and Laura hurried off to answer it, wishing Mr. Don a nice afternoon.

As Mr. Don instructed his driver to get his beach gear and towel, he turned to the table and proceeded to put away his camera. The driver seeing a towel on the hammock, picked it up and placed it in the beach bag.

As the car drove away Laura had finished her phone call and went directly to the hammock, but Bumper was not there nor was his towel. Bumper was on his way to the beach.

There, Mr. Don plopped down in the sand, bought two fresh pineapples which turned out to be a saving grace, for finished with his nap, up sits Bumper wearing his hammock hat. Bumper loves a snack after napping and especially fruit like pineapple, but what a surprise not to wake up in the hammock. After the initial shock and figuring out what happened, they immediately called home. Knowing all was well, everyone began laughing and plans were made to meet for dinner.

Mr. Don had become slightly embarrassed by odd looks from passerby as he shared his lunch, sitting on the beach towel with a rabbit that was wearing a pink hat. Then the tide turned and some of the most beautiful women with kind faces took to Bumper. They wanted to meet him, take him for a hop on the beach and play. Before too long Mr. Don was surrounded with new friends. It was so much fun.

Above the laughter and visiting, Bumper heard a plea for help. He sat upright on his hind legs, head high, ears pointed to the sea. To gain Mr. Don's attention, Bumper began to pound on the sand with his strong back foot.

"What is it boy?" Mr. Don asked

"There is someone in the water, out of control." replied Bumper

They ran to alert the lifeguards. As Mr. Don approached them holding this fluffy rabbit wearing a hat, the lifeguards were not sure if maybe this was a joke, for they could hear nothing. But Bumper has the precious ears, a God given gift and he had to convince these muscle bound lifeguards, which Mr. Don helped greatly with. For he asked them, what have you to lose in taking the boat out to check when there may be a life to be saved?

36

Bumper sat on the helm, upright, giving directions like a captain. He was very happy to be wearing his hat as the sun was blinding. There, pointed Bumper, over the large crested waves was the helpless surfer. Upon reaching shore, crowds had gathered, cheering. The surfer said he prayed a vow to live a better life if he could survive, and thanked Bumper for helping God give him a second chance.

In the setting sun they went home, Mr. Don was much pinker from sunburn.

"How was your day Bumper?" asked Laura

"It was swell, I listened to my instincts," Bumper replied.

LITTLE MISS FISH

Five kittens had been born near the hut of a peasant woman, in the mountains of Ubud. The hut consisted of bamboo poles wedged into the side of a hill with palm leaves on the top, providing relief from the hot sun and tropical rain. The peasant woman thought she was doing what was best for the kittens by giving them her prized possession, a gunny sack. The grateful kittens could chase one another in and out of the gunny sack, jumping and playing, or sleep cuddled inside for warmth.

All was working well until the season changed and the torrential rains arrived swift and hard. The nearby rice fields flooded and the river swelled to the top of its banks. As the rains continued the hillside began to wash away. The bamboo poles gave way and the roof of the hut followed as the water rolled down the hill toward the river. The gunny sack was hit by mud and began to slide down the hill along with the kittens. A tumble, a splash into the river and all swirled away.

All were gone, that is except for one who had gotten snagged by floating twigs downstream. Drifting to the water's edge, this little kitten's head bobbed up and down, she gasped for the breath of life, digging her paws into the muddy bank to claw her way out. There were no houses, just vast fields where she sat in sunlight to dry, dazed by the unexpected and frightened by the unfamiliar surroundings. It didn't seem as if it was supposed to be this way but no one had ever told her otherwise. From this day on, the kitten would always harbor an uncertainty about what life would offer next, taking nothing for granted, anticipating each sunrise as the beginning of a new adventure.

Confidence is built, not through success or failure but by the mere satisfaction of surviving, in this she developed her greatest skill, that of acceptance. Hiding during daylight, with the arrival of darkness she would explore and hunt for sustenance, following the moonlight as a guiding partner. Sleeping in a pile of dried husks would prove to be temporary for the following morning, when she returned they had been burned and this part of the field was now flooded with water for a new planting season. It was time to move on as she learned the cycle of the fields, continuing onward further and further.

Rainy season had begun with hot sporadic downpours as the season progressed, these rains would advance into all day drenching's. Nothing was as beautiful as the garden's glow after one of these washings, as the fragrant, moist soil soaked up the sun. The kitten had found a sanctuary in a private garden just at the edge of a field. Every night she had been entering by jumping the high rock wall and climbing down the mango tree, expressly to observe the other creature that was white and round as a full moon bouncing across the lawn. This she found especially comical and entertaining, having never seen anything like it before, shaking its small head to flop huge ears back and forth. Watching from her hiding place under the shrubbery, the kitten sensed for the first time a delightful joy. Punctually they would both return to this garden knowing that soon their arrival would begin to change like the weather, for neither could risk getting wet from being caught out in the rain.

A dwindling food supply came with the cloud-covered sun, the kitten's fur and body grew thin, for her, warmth no longer existed. Striving each day to simply stay dry, determined to follow her instincts for that is all she had, never considering that by doing what she was supposed to do, she was being brave. But that is exactly what she was, very brave, for there is a time when mere acceptance becomes bravery. Regardless of desires or tribulations, every day taking each circumstance that comes along, responding in accordance by being brave enough to remain true to a divine nature. In that way, remaining exactly as she was meant to be, she was soon rewarded with the best possible life.

On a rainy day she was running hard across the muddy field, it didn't seem fair to have five dogs in pursuit. There at the edge was the garden wall, she sprang upward landing on the ledge, the dogs yipping in frustration, unable to reach that high. As she looked across the field it became clear why they had not caught her, their tracks were deep in the mud, evidence of a slow heavy struggle toward movement. She had left no prints at all, an advantage to being light as a kite although this chase had given her an uncontrollable shivering fear. It was not just the dogs nor the escape, it was the memory from what seemed to be a long time ago, something that made her shiver whenever she got soaking wet. As it continued to downpour there was no place to go for shelter, near the garden was a small house and she did not want to be noticed by the two people on the front porch. It was too late, approaching was a smiling man under an umbrella, she hunched tightly, trying to stay as close to herself as possible, lifted into the palm of his hand. The man's name was

Thomas, he carried the kitten to his wife Laura, saying isn't this the most beautiful little kitten. Wrapping her in a towel to fluff dry, offering warm milk that was refused, they realized she was very shy and not used to being taken care of. A box was placed in a quiet corner of the porch with a blanket and food, the kitten found this acceptable, as the couple stepped away she ate and slept.

There he was, on the floor not far from the box, the deep white fur immensely enhancing an already puffy body. Raising and tilting ears that were independent of one another, even though his eyes were closed the ears were indicative that he knew she was watching. Curiously odd the way his nose twitched as she stepped closer, wanting a better look at this creature that had already been the source of joy in many evenings on the lawn. Nearing, a face that had appeared to be small actually was huge, so were the back feet in comparison to the frail front feet. This disproportionate quality of each feature was the basic charming characteristic of her new friend. The eyes opened, they were tinted a soft pink, in the night they had been glowing a bright red, he possessed night vision like her. In the daylight he was unable to see at all, consequently always napping to avoid bumping into things, his name was Bumper.

Capable is what he had said to her, expressing that he believed her to be capable of leading him every day into the gardens where they could explore together. Long before she arrived, he had spent leisurely afternoons planning adventures while alone on the porch. Now the opportunity was presented to experience that which both desired, the honor of a trusting bond.

It was this wise rabbit that understood the kitten's craving for fish, which she always devoured rapidly. A serving of fresh-ocean catch had been the first meal that was ever prepared especially for her, providing a tremendous sense of wellbeing. Under no circumstances was she prepared to allow the risk of losing that feeling. She began preserving it by only wanting fish, conveying her appreciation by responding to the name Fish. Under Bumper's advice, that it would be acceptable to eat another food that is not a favorite since fish would not always be available for supper, he said you may miss fish but you will only a "little miss fish" since there will be other choices such as beef or chicken. Between the two of them her name became Little Miss Fish and only they ever knew the exact meaning.

Just when she thought he had taught her everything, he would come up with something new, teaching reading, writing, but not arithmetic. Arithmetic is not something that needed to be taught, everyone knew that two by two is four and four by four is a whole lot more. Writing was performed with the chin, by rubbing against the steps up the porch or on the corner of the house. Reading that is what was important, learning to read the stars and the leaves of a tree, after all the world revolves on an axis of a pencil, which is used to send messages in nature.

Together they began to explore, each sharing their own understanding of the natural world. On the premise of friendship their adventures began.

"Oh Fish not really, weren't you scared?" asked Bumper.

"I never think of myself as being scared, only protective," replied Fish.

"Then why do you always run and hide whenever we have visitors, I thought you were being a scaredy cat," said Bumper.

"Not me Bumper, I am never scared, anyway I didn't know you noticed things like that since you are always picked up and poked at when company arrives," replied Fish.

"Well they would like to poke at you too if you weren't so scared and always hiding," Bumper replied.

"I already told you it is not that I am scared, I don't just run off and hide. It just so happens that I have important things to do, I am very busy. Too busy doing important things like maintaining my dignity. Imagine how silly it would be for me if I allowed a perfect stranger to tug at my ears the way they do with you. No thank you indeed, I would rather stay on schedule doing my important things. I am busy you know, very busy. I do have important busy things to do," explained Fish.

"Yes, I have noticed you are a very important cat, my dear friend Fish. Many times while I am in the yard napping I think how good it is to have Miss Fish on duty so that I can rest knowing nothing can get past Fish. That's why you really should not stay out all night. We all sleep so much better when you come in the house for the night at ten o'clock like you're supposed to. I still think you must have been just a little frightened in the dark last night all by yourself," stated Bumper.

48

"Perhaps that's the answer, I wasn't exactly all by myself, not that I would have been frightened anyway, even if I were alone. You must know by now that I am fearless, positively fearless. Remember the lion, king of the jungle is a cat, I am a cat. Fearless, Bumper, positively fearless," explained Fish.

"Oh yes Fish, I would never forget that your cat family is royalty in the jungle, and rightfully so I might add. I knew that before I was born, even before you told me," said Bumper. "What did you mean when you said perhaps that's the answer?" Bumper asked.

"Oh Bumper, concentrate, it was the second part that was important. I said I wasn't exactly alone. There was a full moon, a full moon Bumper, I know I should not stay out all night and I don't intend to make a habit of it. This was one of those rare moments when one has no choice in the matter. One of those important things to do. You may not believe me but I tell you the truth, our yard never became dark, not totally that is. The light from above in our heavens lasted all night long," explained Fish.

"Not really, how could it be? Are you sure you didn't just fall asleep and wake up at sunrise?" Bumper asked.

"Impossible, fall asleep with all the excitement. It was – It was indescribable," said Fish.

Bumper nodded off to sleep as did Fish. She was tired from being out all night. Bumper began to think about this word indescribable. Fish was so smart, she always knew the big words. Indescribable, he thought to himself, sounded rather delicious. He didn't realize it was getting close to dinner time, that's why he was thinking of eating again. So, he decided to try some excitement for himself, which sounded so delicious. Yes, he decided to stay out that night. Oh, it will be so much fun. In all his days and nights outside in the garden, he had never really been alone. Once in a while he was almost alone, this he knew because he was by himself but only for a short while. In that time he would explore, finding the new bamboo shoots, chewing them down to size. Measure the length of the kangkung vine, chopping it off so it wouldn't get to long and grow over his path. Rub his chin on every low branch, since he could not see well in the daylight, he would know it was there the next time he passed by. He knew his garden, he knew it well. If there was something new and delicious to be found at night, then he was determined to be there. Ten o'clock came, time to bring in Fish, and when the door opened, Bumper dashed out, hiding under the table on the patio. Fish hesitated at the door seeing Bumper's escape and wondered if anyone else noticed. She was going to go over to Bumper but he began to shake his head right to left with his big floppy ears falling from side to side, no Fish, no. Fish was picked up, she looked into Laura's eyes and meowed softly, sweetly meowed. "Oh my sweet kitty, time for bed," said Laura.

Fish lay on the end of the bed with her eyes on the door. *Oh dear*, she thought, *what is Bumper up to now?* Surely he wouldn't be planning to stay out all night, not on a dark night like this, with no moon. He can see perfectly clear with no light at all. Still it is very foolish considering all the hunters and him with no camouflage. He can be seen for miles with his shiny white fur. No way he could hide well enough not to be found, what to do? What, oh what to do?

Bumper didn't waste any time hopping across the porch to the steps where he looked out into his yard, there was no light from above as Fish said. He sat on top of the steps, ears upright swiveling in each direction. Picking up no sound other than crickets, he went down the steps. Two hops, stop, check for sound, three hops, stop, check again. Look left, look right, nothing, further and further into his yard sniffing, listening. His paws were getting wet from the lawn, beginning to feel cold. Must find the indescribable, where could it be? Onward, but where?

Something skittered across the rocks in front of him. Rocks!! He had already reached the rock edge at the far end, an area he was not familiar with, in fact he considered it outside of his garden zone. Large dark shrubs rustled, he braced with face low, ears stretched. A bat flew overhead dropping a half-eaten apple that landed with a thud. Startled, Bumper ran, suddenly the little front paws were getting pinched, sliding into crevices of rock. Ouch, Rocks! Unsure why he ran, as nothing seemed to be chasing him, so where he was, he stopped to take a survey, and then he saw the apple. "That could have been a close call, I almost got hit on the head with an apple," he said. It must be Baxter. "Baxter is that you? Baxter," Bumper called.

"Yes Bumper," said the bat while hanging upside down in a nearby palm tree. "Sorry you were startled. I was so surprised to find you out that I dropped my supper and then with my radar, I could sense you dashing and darting about. Love to hang around but I must soar the night away. By the way, that pesky cat of yours isn't out is she?" Before Bumper could answer Baxter had gone.

Bumper watched his friend fly off tilting this way and that way, appearing to disappear when really he was still there. Baxter the bat looked rather old fashioned, as if he were wearing a cape. When the cape was open, the bat possessed the night or did the night possess the bat? Bumper wasn't sure. As if Baxter was like a vapor that became part of the wind, the dark wind of night.

Swoosh, Baxter clutched the underside of a long palm leaf in a tree close to where Bumper was. He had gotten himself another apple and was eating it with precision. His front arms had long fingers that could hold and turn the fruit for each bite. He actually ate while hanging upside down. It was a small, pink, waxy apple that grew wild, Bumper was fond of those himself.

"I could get you an apple Bumper, but really you shouldn't just sit there in those rocks much longer. Sly has been spotted coming down the fence line, no doubt he will pass this way," Baxter advised.

As much as Bumper wanted one of those apples the thought of Sly the snake coming up behind him gave him the jitters. He had lost his appetite, something that had never happened before. Finding the indescribable was no longer a priority, he must get back to the shrubs at the front porch where there was safety and warmth. "No thanks," he said to Baxter, "I'm going home now."

Looking out across the lawn, feeling it would be a long way back, Bumper came up with a strategy. From that night on it would be referred to as hop-n-halt. When one does not know from which direction danger comes, it is best to proceed slowly, one hop at a time. It seemed to take forever just to reach half way. Bumper didn't mind, he was being entertained between hops by the twinkling of the many stars shining on this night. As he gazed skyward he noticed in the distance a mass of bats all dropping apples. Must be a bad batch of apples he thought. Finally arriving successfully into the front shrubs, he waited for sunrise.

In the morning he realized that the sound of the front door opening filled him with such a joy that it was indescribable. He had found it after all, at his own front door. Fish was eager to hear all about his adventure but Bumper had fallen asleep, only saying that he had been busy doing important busy things. So that night at sunset when the bats came out Fish would find Baxter and he would tell her just what went on.

"Hello Fish," said Baxter. "We have all decided that if it has to be one or the other of you out, we would prefer it be you. From the air that rabbit looked like a full moon sitting on the lawn all night long. We had to pick an entire tree of apples and bombard Sly, just so that he would take a detour and not find your friend. None of us can figure out why Bumper would take so long to get across the lawn! Out of our respect for you, we kept him safe."

"Thanks Baxter," said Fish. "You can fly through our porch any time with no more disturbances from me."

CRYING TREE
STORY OF LUWAK

In the dark jungle forest under stars on a moonlit night, everything seems to be a shade of gray, even the green leaves. In this grayness, it is difficult to recognize the figures that appear to be shadows moving between and around the tall palms that stand as iron rods. Size and shape is distorted, unable to see distinguishing features, one animal may look like another. These are the creatures that sleep during day's heat, entering the cool night air to hunt or steal. It can be risky for them if they are caught while they are stealing. Other animals will attack and the thieves will be severely injured, sometimes killed. It is very dangerous to be a thief.

Bumper and Fish would never steal, they watch the shadows crossing the lawn from their garden near the jungle. Most are small creatures that make squeaky sounds when they get startled. Large animals have the advantage in an attack if they remain unseen when stalking a fat rabbit like Bumper, so Miss Fish takes great pride in her keen observations to help keep her friend safe by staying close to him. She, after all, is the small jungle cat, an expert in the stealth of a hunt.

Bumper is on the grass in the light of a full moon, he is playing. Kicking both back feet high, he runs a short distance, skids to a stop, turns quickly and runs back. Several times he does this, sometimes shaking his ears back and forth as he runs. Fish, who had been sitting, now crouches low to the ground, in a quick trot races for the porch, at the same time Bumper has stood upright. His small front paws hanging loosely, his wide ears on alert. Giving the signal, he pounds the ground hard with his long back foot and sprints up the steps with Fish, they are safe.

Both study the creature now in their yard, they are puzzled. It looks like a huge gray rat as big as a dog with a long nose and tail. They thought its boldness might indicate it had been hunting them. As it crosses the lawn exactly where they had just been, they can see the long, thick, gray fur. It is Luwak, a rare jungle cat, the size and shape of a fox. Everyone knows she is a thief that steals eggs from a nearby farm. Her steady pace takes her out of the moon lit lawn into the tree-covered darkness where she usually stays. Luwak moves like a cat with determination, as if she has a plan. She lives across the river in the hollow of an ancient tree. It was quite by accident that Bumper and Fish found her home one day, they made a promise to keep the location a secret.

This tree, on the far side of the river, deep in the jungle, is old and wide and it has not many branches, these few reach straight up skyward. Only the very top of the branches have green leaves for a short period of time in the year. Around its base in the moss covered ground, grow tall damp ferns. This is the Crying Tree, home to Luwak, a well-kept secret in the jungle. Over the recent years several of these trees have begun to sing their own crying song. A haunting mystery to those that do not know the voice of the tree comes from within. For those that do understand, the beauty of hearing more than one tree cry is a blessing.

Luwak lives in the hollow of this dead-looking tree. The opening was above ground, once inside she sleeps below the opening. To pass by and look in, you would see nothing. In evenings when it was cold or rainy, Luwak comforts her hunger by singing a sorrowful melody. Since there are vicious thieves that will steal her from her forest home by trapping, caging, and using her in the production of coffee, she is not able to enter the light of day to find food without risk of being captured, seeking her nourishment under the protection of nighttime's darkness. During the season of torrential rains, nights are too wet and she must go without food, sometimes for several days. The pain of hunger she knows well. The loneliness of suffering as the number of those free as nature intended, dwindled each year, she does not understand. Hidden deep within the tree, she spoke in the universal voice. Neither a howl nor a whimper, rather a long mournful song that was carried throughout the forest in the wet wind, making it impossible to find the location from where it came. A song taunting anyone whom should listen. "I may be the last, hear my hunger, I hunger for life," over and over again, hour after hour, lulling herself to sleep.

The air is heavy with mist, all color is gray. There are clouds covering the vastness above, eliminating the hint of a sparkling star. The rippling river will cling to her voice as a messenger sending it throughout the forest miles downstream. The wind will embrace each note of distress claiming it as its own, "hear my hunger, I hunger for life." Through the branches that grasp toward heaven, it is the tree as an instrument standing as a cathedral pipe organ that will magnify Luwak's mournful song into a haunting echo. Expelling it directly into the spirit nation of God. The significance of the few leaves at the tippy top is that they look like fingers reaching to grab hold of heaven in an effort to pull itself upward, entering through the sheer brute strength of desire. Hanging on, never to let go, taking with it Luwak, for there is always a place for her in the heart of the crying tree.

Bumper and Fish hear this cry as a warning. That if she is not able to find nourishment soon she might not survive. Many areas of the jungle have already lost their precious Luwak forever. One more would be a disaster for all. This creature is at such a great risk of being stolen that it has to hide all day. In the rainy season, nights are always wet, increasing the odds against her survival.

The next day Bumper and Fish were worried, as Bumper said, "This is of great magnitude." A word he liked to use when he wanted to be taken seriously.

Fish reminded Bumper that Luwak is a thief in night, raiding the chicken farms. "Yes" said Bumper, "my stronger feeling is that she is starving and although that is no excuse for stealing, in her hunger we may find a solution."

"I quite agree, if only she would hunger for honesty," said Fish. "Her mournful cry is haunting me and yet if I don't hear it, I worry that I may never hear it again. That she may be gone forever."

"If Luwak goes who is next?" asked Bumper. "Who is next?"

"To save a thief, what will our neighbors say? No one likes a thief, stealing is not proper behavior," said Fish. "Even if we could help, how would we? That's the bigger problem."

"You mean the bigger part of the same problem. A problem can have many parts. The more parts the bigger the problem and parts are small problems. So we must solve many small problems. That way there are no parts left to make a big problem. That will be our plan, agreed?" asked Bumper.

"I can always count on your being clever" answered Fish. "That makes it very clear for me. We need to think of all our small problems and as each one is corrected the big one will disappear. The more small parts we can solve the smaller the problem becomes."

Just then Bumper pounded the ground with his large hind foot and dashed for cover into the purple flowered heather that surrounded his garden. Fish crouched low as she saw Sly the snake coming their way. She started swatting at it, reaching out her paw with the claws extended.

Sly said, "Ouch, quit stabbing me with your sharp toes."

Fish asked, "Where are you going? You really shouldn't come through our yard."

Sly answered, "I'm going to the river to visit the rat. There are a group of geese in the brush that won't let me pass so I had to come this way."

"Geese," said Fish, "what are they doing there?"

"I heard that their owners moved," said Sly, "and left them to find their own way. Now they are lost and making a squawking sound that I cannot stand to listen to."

Fish darted off to find Bumper. He was still hiding from the snake. "Sly's gone Bumper, and all our small problems are resolved," said Fish. "That is, if you would like to have geese living in our pond." She told Bumper how the snake would not tolerate the squawk of geese and if the geese lived in the pond there would be no more snakes.

"Bumper said he wasn't sure he liked the squawk either but he much preferred it to snakes. Let's invite them to live here, do you think they will come?"

"We can offer protection for them Bumper, that is with Luwak's help, she is out all night when they like to sleep. All the geese have to do is provide extra eggs. It is a win-win for everyone, the best of all solutions."

It was easy for them to find the geese. They were still making loud noises and thrashing their wings in the thick brush. The idea of a cool, calm pond was exactly what they wanted. A new home, and what better neighbors than Bumper and Fish? As for the eggs, no problem, there were five geese always with extra eggs. They were however unsure about being protected by a Luwak. Fish explained, "The eggs are a trade and not to be stolen. Luwak would no longer be a thief and so she would only take what she is entitled to. A friend to all the night creatures, she will tell them of her arrangement with you, she can protect you well, believe me. I should think that by tomorrow the entire jungle would have heard this news." So it was settled.

Bumper's ears started twitching as he was listening to Fish. His ears twitched when he wanted to say something but didn't think he should. Anyway, right at the moment he was busy chewing through the small branches to help the geese on their way. They were eager to reach the pond, it was bigger than they expected, and grateful, they hurried off.

Fish knew the twitching ear signal, she asked, "What's with your ears?"

"It's just that – that the plan is perfect, except something about it is bothering me," said Bumper.

"That's not a good sign, now you've got me worried, what could it possibly be that may go wrong?" asked Fish.

"Something that was already happening before we thought of the plan. Fish, it is not raining anymore and I cannot hear the crying tree."

Just then they heard a loud scream followed by barking. A pack of dogs were chasing something and they were running toward the pond. It was Luwak, she fell from a bite in the leg. Just as the three dogs were ready to attack her again the geese began flapping their wings and squawking. This surprised the dogs just long enough for Luwak to make a run for it around to the other side of the pond. Bumper and Fish gave the dogs another distraction. Then they realized that geese could be quite fierce themselves as they saw them chasing the dogs away yipping. The geese, the cat, and the rabbit went to find Luwak. She was in the tall ferns where she had slipped with her injured leg.

The geese paddled up to her and said, "Thank you, thank you, we didn't expect you so soon but now we know how valuable you are for us. We are so sorry you got hurt trying to protect us."

Luwak didn't know what to say. She was hurt, she was hungry, and she was scared. She was just about to get angry with them, she would try to pretend she was not hurt to defend herself. They must be crazy, she had been caught at the farmers stealing eggs, not defending them.

"Luwak," said Fish, "the geese have eggs for you, they would like you to come every night. They would be so grateful for your help in keeping them safe."

Then she recognized Bumper and Fish. She knew them from a distance, occasionally seeing the two near the large tree where she lived. There was no fear of these two, in fact often she had admired their friendship with each other and now they admired her as a skilled defender. With her stealthy almond eyes roving from one to the other, Luwak made one of the most difficult decisions of her life. At this moment she would define her future as a friend, by telling them the truth and risk losing that which she most desired, acceptance. To prepare herself for the worst she stood up, her back leg quivering in pain, whether to run or snarl would depend on their reaction.

The big goose paddled up to her saying, "Luwak, you must not do any more tonight, stay off your leg. Let us put a mudpack on the wound." Then he turned to the medium goose ordering eggs to be brought to their new friend.

Still standing, Luwak said, "You must know I have lived my past as a thief and that on this dusk, that is what I was doing."

Fish turned to Bumper and said, "She certainly is cunning isn't she. I hope we have not underestimated her. I do believe she is determined to have those eggs one way or another."

It was Bumper whose tender little heart felt for Luwak. He saw she was at her most vulnerable, usually hunting in the dark, it was not quite dark yet. Injured, she would not be able to hunt this night, already hungry because this was rainy season, it may have been days before it was dry enough for her to find food. Yet here she remained, clever and crafty with her dignity intact.

"Yes," Bumper said to Fish, "we did underestimate her. She is truly remarkable, truly." He then stepped closer to Luwak and spoke very quietly. "You are not your past; you are walking out of it." Luwak felt Bumper's kindness and wisdom, she was unarmed.

"Like I said," spoke up the big goose, "we had not expected you so early. Now let's get that leg healed." Putting mud on his wide bill, the goose applied it to the wound which turned out to be only a one-tooth puncture. The mud felt cool as it dried, the wound would heal rapidly. Eggs, eggs, and more, nice big goose eggs took the dizziness from Luwak's head as she ate. The geese seemed to all be talking at once, "Tomorrow," they said, "If we are asleep when you arrive don't wake us up just help yourself."

There was too much noise for Luwak. She wanted to tell them they had saved her, she did not get the chance, for Bumper said "Thank-you for your honesty. Deceiving is theft, it is stealing the truth from someone, which you did not do. You stood in your own truth with courage, prepared to accept the consequences, that is integrity. We would be proud for you to accept us as your friend."

"And I the same," said Luwak, the beautiful rare jungle cat limped away to home, her crying tree silent on this night.

Bumper and Fish also left for home, the geese went to sleep. On the way home Bumper said, "It's too bad we couldn't have explained to her first."

"It all turned out okay, mission accomplished," answered Fish as she trotted on.

"Didn't you see how confused she was?" asked Bumper, trying to keep up with her fast pace.

"What I saw is that she is crafty, she nearly slipped away." replied Fish.

"Yes, haven't we all Fish, haven't we all." Bumper said.

WOMAN OF DUST

There are times when Fish says to me, "Come on Bumper, the journey begins."

On a day we were outside in the yard it all started. I was in the shady clover patch under a large tree. Fish was in the tree imitating the various birdcalls, one of her favorite games, when she saw someone coming down our road. Just about the same time I heard the footsteps of bare feet on dirt. That wasn't the sound of danger but we both felt there was the possibility of danger. Fish lowered her body into the tree where she had been sitting, now she was camouflaged by leaves and branches. I pounded the ground hard with my huge back foot to make sure Fish stayed hidden, and I ran to hide myself in a hole under the exposed roots.

Approaching steadily was a very old woman, approximately the age of Earth. Her clothes, hair and skin were all the same color as dust. The color one takes on when you live and age as the dust of Earth, blending into the world. The closer she came the more frightened we were. As she passed by, we realized the danger was not for us but for the contents of a cloth sack that hung over her bent back. Weak little sounds came from that sack, sounds of confusion and weariness. The woman appeared to be frail, walking slowly down our road to a path that only leads toward the river. Continuing to watch her, we could see she was not far away, yet because of her color she almost seemed to disappear.

Fish jumped off the high tree branch using her tail to balance a perfect landing on the ground in front of me. We both agreed that the old woman was like a cloud of dust and maybe she would blow away right in front of our eyes, if there were a big wind. I was relieved that she drifted on past with that scary sack.

"We are going to watch that sack," said Fish, "we are not going to let it out of our sight!"

"Have you forgotten I'm nocturnal, I don't see well at all in all this daylight? How can I possibly not let something out of my sight that was never in my sight?" I asked.

"There is nothing about you Bumper that I would ever forget. You do possess spectacular hearing with those extraordinary ears and I know you didn't like what you heard. It's not the sack that is scary it's the fear of being trapped as contents," Fish explained. "Come on Bumper, the journey begins, we have got to catch up with her."

We went into the bushes alongside the path and made haste to follow the dust-like creature of a woman. That is how our journey began, not planned or prepared for. Just two friends on an adventure in trust and companionship.

Fish trotted off at a quick pace with her tail in the air, determined to reach the river's edge, before it was too late. I was hopping alongside her, trying to keep up, it wasn't easy. Where Fish's slender body could slip through an area, I would have to chew through. Snapping off twigs and small branches to make the opening big enough for my round body. Half way into a dense patch of shrubbery I realized I was half way stuck.

Fish saw my predicament, "Don't panic," she said. "Just back up!"

Yes, she was right, follow the half that is not stuck. I wiggled myself backwards while Fish found a route I could take under the shrubs. It just required a little extra digging.

"Hurry up Bumper, we don't want to be too late," she said.

Since Fish was just sitting there watching me dig a tunnel, I thought it would be a good chance for her to tell me just exactly what it was we didn't want to be late for.

Fish said, "A sack going toward the river is not a good thing, it has a way of getting loose, slipping, sliding and tumbling until it plops into the river. If that happens we have to be there, that fresh clear water is too strong and cold for little creatures."

Bumper shivered at the thought of being submerged in cold water, he didn't even like to get his feet wet for fear of catching a chill. Finally he had burrowed under the shrubbery, he was not paying attention and tripped, rolling into a pile of dry leaves. His long fur had been silky white when they left, now it was soiled and matted with tattered leaves, the innocent pink cloudy eyes held tears.

"Are you hurt?" asked Fish as she helped brush off his fur.

"Only in my heart, it makes me sad to think of little unaware creatures tumbling down into unknown depths," said Bumper.

Fish gave him encouragement by saying, "Sad things happen to everyone sometime. When I fell into the river I survived, but I am a tri colored cat and a tri colored cat is lucky. Not only that, I found a home with you and learned love by being loved. I just want the creatures in that sack to have the same opportunity; we have to get them free before they get wet from the river."

Bumper was trying to come up with a plan, considering all the possibilities. "What about the woman of dust, she must be very mean, doesn't she know how cold that water is? Maybe she will catch us and throw us in the river or try to chase us to the end of our day."

"We don't concern ourselves with her, just think about that sack," ordered Fish. "Anyway she might not be mean, for all we know maybe she thinks they will have a better life downstream. A lot of people are not very smart, no reason to think she is."

Thick ferns were easy passage and it meant they had reached the river. Under the long fern fronds sat the two friends, shoulder to shoulder, peering out onto the path, spying on the woman of dust, who was sitting on a large gray river boulder. It was a quick flowing river, except in this one spot where there were many big rocks slowing down the current to create a shallow pool of water. This was considered the safest area should one need to cross. A place for animals to get a cool drink in the warm evening or to sun on the rocks in a fresh morning light. This place had real fish, river rats, and best of all, no wild dogs.

The woman of dust was opening her sack of kittens in distress, singing to them as she reached deep inside to lift them out one by one. Bumper thought it was a chant but Fish said no, that is a special song only cats understand, *meong meong meong*.

Continuing her song to comfort the little kittens before placing them on her lap she kissed the top of each little head. They were all colors of her. Different tones of grays and browns all mixed up together like dust. They all seemed to be the same as one. No spaces between seeing where one began and the other began. The sack, the boulder, the river, the woman, the kittens, were all the same color, we saw a simple shade of life.

We could smell the smoke from an extinguished campfire and the aroma of supper. The woman unrolled a boiled fish from a piece of paper, taking out the bones, using the paper as a mat on her lap for the kittens to eat the meat. She ate a hard-boiled egg, adding the crumbled up shell to a cup of hot coffee. As the kittens tumbled in play she watched, fluffing the sack filling it with dried leaves to prepare a bed, wedging it into the ferns. Placing each of the kittens onto their fresh bed, saying "bless us all," and they all lay down together. At that moment she looked directly to where Bumper and Fish were hiding. They were no longer afraid of her, for the first time they had met her eyes and there was kindness. As if speaking to them, she said, "Bless you all, little ones."

"Should we say God bless you to?" whispered Bumper to Fish.

"No, we're still hiding," said Fish. "They sure had a good meal didn't they? I'm hungry, let's go home."

"Yeah, me too. Looks like we are going to have some new neighbors to meet if they decide to stay," said Bumper.

"I don't think we can count on them being here very long. Dust has a way of disappearing as quickly as it appears. Anyway, this day has been very important for me, I met with charity in that woman of dust. Come on, we'll take the path home," said Fish.

Oh good! Bumper knew that was faster than trying to plough through the bushes again.

The two friends trotted and hopped together side by side, reaching home before sunset. On the way Fish said "I really wanted to save those kittens, I was ready to save those kittens and now I'm a little disappointed that I didn't get to." Bumper twitched an ear toward her, he was tired from a long day, deciding that tomorrow he would tell her how brave she was for taking the chance. But for now he would speak in his simple wisdom, saying, "It is not in the saving that we will sleep tonight. It is in the knowing they are safe that we will sleep in peace."

Home was not so far away. They had been on a journey throughout the day.

On A Journey Through The Bushes Along A Path
To Where The River Bends
Taking Only Our Bravery Together We Went
Me And My Friend

There We Saw The Woman Of Dust
Upon Her Lap Three Kittens Sweet
All Were A Shade Of Gray As Was The River And
The Rocks Beneath Her Feet

We Had To Blink Once Or Twice We Could
Barely
Believe Our Eyes
The Surrounding Color She Summoned Gave Her
A Disappearing Disguise

Natures Way Of Blending Tones So That They

Were All As One

Just As Earth Is To Dust Or As In A Rainy Days

Cloud Covered Sun

We Had Been Too Late The Campfire Had
Already
Been Put Out

Boiled Fish And Egg They Ate And Coffee With

Sugar No Doubt

The Kittens Played As Kittens Do While She Sang

To Their Delight

Then She Kissed Them On The Head With A

Blessing

For A Good Night

Nature Met Her Everywhere This Woman Of Dust

In Kindness Not Strife

We Met Charity In A Color Common To

Everyone

A Simple Shade Of Life

FIRE CLOUDS

It could not have been a more perfect day. Early to rise, Fish was eager to see the sun. Clouds were in the sky but not visible as such, the edges of which were glowing like flames as they outlined a large hot pink circle casting a fiery glow.

"Spectacular, get up Bumper, you must come and see this glorious sunrise," said Fish.

Slowly Bumper stretched, opening his mouth to a full-fledged yawn. He hopped to the end of his bench looking for the piece of carrot he left for that moment. He heard Fish again saying, "Hurry up, it's rising fast, you're going to miss it."

Fish was sitting on the porch, hollering to Bumper without taking her eyes off what she had never seen before in the sky. Sunrise yes, many times, but nothing like this one. Suddenly it dawned on Bumper, he was now awake and when he couldn't find the carrot he had decided it was time to go out for breakfast anyway. He was glad Fish kept telling him time to get up, he was hungry. What is it this time she is persisting about? Sunrise she had said, a special sunrise.

Bumper ran back and forth on his bench to draw attention to the fact that he was ready to be put on the floor. He was not able to see well enough to jump down by himself so every morning Thomas or Laura would give him a helping hand. This morning Thomas was nearest, so he had the privilege of lifting Bumper and receiving a good morning smile. With little or no light at all Bumper can see better than most. So in the morning just as the sun was peeking over the rounded curve of earth and not full enough to create a glare of light, Bumper could find his way to the porch.

"Bumper, look, it's a sunrise, you can see. You can see it can't you? The clouds, look at the clouds," exclaimed Fish.

He stood beside Fish and gazed skyward. He had heard stories of such a morning that happened before his parents were born. Could it, could it possibly be? Is this the Fire Cloud my Grandy knew?

"What did you say Bumper? Bumper you do see it don't you?"

"Yes, oh yes Fish." Bumper answered feeling more than a little uneasy. He had to make certain that what he thought he saw was actually there. He fell silent.

"I am so glad you can see it too," said Fish. "I have never seen anything like it."

By now you could see the full shadow of the sun, the color remained pink. It was inside the cloud. The outer edges of this cloud were uneven and bright red.

"It's a signal, Fish, from the grand council of the highest nature. When the sun and the clouds become one in cooperation, they make big plans and I am bound by duty and honor to be of assistance."

"What is this you are talking about now? I have never heard of such nonsense," Fish said. She was sure Bumper must be mistaken. How could a small creature like Bumper think he could be of any service in the grand plans of the universe?

"Then you have not heard about fire clouds," Bumper answered. "It all began with a rabbit by the name of Grandy."

"Grandy," Fish said. "No, I have not met Grandy. Where does he sleep?"

"That's a good question, Fish. I have never actually met him myself. But I can tell you I know him because there is a little grandness in all rabbits. Grandy was one of the first rabbits and he witnessed just such a sunrise. It was toward the end of rainy season, like now. All the boroughs were wet, some actually filled beyond capacity with water. You know how it is, Fish, when a rabbit's fur gets wet, it starts to fall out. There were rabbits with nearly no fur at all. Can you imagine how big my ears would look if I were not rounded to fullness with fur?"

"I can imagine, Bumper, but I do not want to think about no fur, why, the idea is practically indecent, not to mention cold. The poor rabbits. Where could they possibly go to get warm?" Fish asked.

"Let me tell you the legend of Grandy," answered Bumper.

The rabbits asked the sun for warmth but the sun, it was also cold, even the sun shivered day and night as the rain continued. The rabbits and sun, began to make plans. The rabbits could arrange with birds, to give the sun more fuel so it would burn hotter. Birds were sent to drop twigs and leaves on the sun but these were too wet to burn and the twigs and leaves laid on the sun like rubbish, making it heavy and that much slower to rise. It was then decided the rabbits would have to request Mr. Wind to blow the rubbish off. This would require wolves, wolves speak every night to the wind, but who can speak to wolves? Surely not rabbits, because rabbits and wolves are not exactly on friendly terms.

"A cloud could speak to the wolves," said Grandy. The wolves were also cold and wet, they especially do not like getting wet because that is like taking a bath. Wolves never bathe, they like to be smelly. But they were well fed since the rains had flooded the homes, most animals were left without shelter. The wolves grew fat and lazy.

"They are not hungry enough to eat something they are not sure of," said Grandy. "I will go disguised as a cloud to speak with the wolves." He tied his ears under his chin so the wolves would not recognize him as a rabbit. He was pure white, and at that time and place he was the only white rabbit.

"Bumper, what about the hopping?" asked Fish. The big back hoppers could be seen.

"Yes Fish, I am getting there, as the legend continues," answered Bumper.

Ducks, quack quack waddle waddle, ducks. They liked the puddles of water but they already had enough water before the rains, now there was so much it was difficult to find a dry place for their eggs. So they were more than willing to help Grandy and play a trick on the wolves. But they were not to quack and waddle, this was part of the secret plan. Ducks are very good at keeping a secret, except not among themselves. They gossip all day in groups, then one group will go to the next and in a short amount of time there is nothing they don't all know about. That's how they found the duck who could hold his air the longest while swimming underwater. Grandy sat on top of the duck and appeared to be floating down the river near the edge where the wolves lay.

"Who go there? Who be you?" snarled one wolf after another.

"I be Cloud Smell Good," said Grandy. The creatures around about the shrubs and trees nearly gave away the whole plan in trying not to laugh out loud. Grandy continued to float closer and closer.

"Smell good elsewhere," barked the wolves.

"I would if I could," said Grandy, "but Cloud Smell Good listens only to Mr. Wind, I am under his command. I go where the wind blows nearest the sun."

The duck whispered to Grandy, "You are sounding too smart. Speak stupid or these wolves will never figure out what to do. Make it clear, and quickly."

It started to rain and Grandy felt a sneeze coming on. He had to hold it back, for if he should sneeze, his ears would come untied and the whole plan would be ruined.

"Home for you is not here, we want no more smell good," barked the wolves.

Grandy answered "Smell Good lives in the sun, should the wind blow there I will go. Oh brave wolves speak to Mr. Wind."

"Ah friend wind. Ah friend wind," the wolves howled and howled in unison.

Rains fell hard and the wind was blowing so strong, that branches and twigs were flying to earth from every direction. The wolves were running for cover and did not notice the duck paddling quickly downstream for escape with Cloud Smell Good sneezing on his back. Every creature was still wet when a patch of blue sky appeared. The clouds were moving swiftly across the earth, casting shadow paths of darkness until all the clouds lifted up to the sun. The sun was covered in a vapor of clouds and this must have warmed the sun. The next morning at sunrise it started to glow a bright pink and the edges of the clouds were flaming fire. Fire clouds were born. They live in the sun and help to complete each season.

"Unless they become visible like today and then those of us that know, must, by duty and honor heed the signal," said Bumper.

"That includes me, Bumper," said Fish, "Because now I know. What is it I know Bumper, what is it we do when we see the signal, what does it mean?"

"It means there is some concern in the universe. We are part of the plan, the grand plan as it is called, named after my Grandy. As for the doing what. The doing is in the knowing. Knowing what to do. So in a way we are doing by knowing because as of yet there is nothing we know to do. Maybe what we are supposed to do is to know and since we know, now we are done. We know we are willing and sometimes the pure nature of wanting to help and being ready to help is all that is required. Together Fish, we stay ready. We do what we know and we know what we do. Fire Clouds do the same, they signal that the grand plan is under council with the clouds and the sun and the wind and we stand ready in knowing," explained Bumper.

Bumper and Fish sat on the porch side by side, both bravely ready to face whatever should come their way.

BIG RAIN DAY

On this day, the day of the big rain, it wasn't just another wet rainy day. Today there weren't raindrops like usual. Today it rained puddles. Puddles of water instead of drops. The sky was full of falling puddles. Puddle after puddle fell on our park as we watched the grass disappear until it was completely under water, looking more like a lake than a park. What could we do except just lay on the porch watching our entire afternoon of play sink away.

Then just as quickly as it started, it stopped. The air was still wet but we could see the sun again, its heat drew the moisture from the ground upward until even the tallest tree was breathing steam. The leaves became weighted and droopy as sprinkles of rain fell off and on, unexpectedly. When the air became cooled, in came a gust of wind bending the trees as it pushed through the branches on its way out to sea. Fish and I saw leaves falling but before they landed on the ground this gust of

98

wind had gone. We looked at each other in amazement, we both knew immediately this was the swift and fierce wind named Old Gust, the leader of all the wind that would follow in short intervals throughout the day. From our porch we watched and listened as the wind began to howl. As the life of each gust that passed, blew its breath into our waiting ears, filling our nose with recognition. Swirling in a dance in front of our eyes, as if turning to take a second look before continuing onward to gather with Old Gust near the ocean's beach. On that beach of black sand, there was some grand plan in action that only the wind knew about. In a hurry for miles across water and land this wind came to become part of something greater together than each gust could possibly be alone. A force of life filled with the understanding that its purpose is honorable and nothing could prevent this wind from performing its duty. It would blow you over or sting to get you out of its way.

Commanding respect, Old Gust had never stopped whenever he passed through our yard but Fish knew Old Gust from before. On one occasion she had been in a tree and there out of nowhere suddenly appeared Old Gust. In his direction he made an abrupt turn to avoid her perch so she would not be blown out of her tree. She had always wanted to thank him for this kindness but his dignity would never allow her to catch up with his haste. That is the mystery about Old Gust and the other gusts brushing across our face or hair, always moving, even when it is gone you know it is only somewhere else arriving just as quickly as it goes. Maybe today Fish could take the risk to finally speak her gratitude to Old Gust. For on this day there seemed to be an opportunity with the wind lingering in an area that it now claimed, the vast domain of the ocean. She took the chance with me by her side, leaving our safe porch to trot around the edge of our flooded park and through our gated wall.

The sun was unwilling to participate, it began to hide above the gray clouds that were being pushed in a race by gust after gust. Irregular shapes of cloud were being stacked and positioned, creating a sight barrier by mixing with flying sand grit. Leaping waves of salt water were slapped over and over until the ocean was like a thunderous rolling piece of machinery, but it wasn't a machine, it was alive. Salted sand thrown into the air stung our eyes, we were ready to go home but the way was no longer visible. Old Gust was there but his energy was far too intense for us to venture close.

This was a gathering of forces, an event that was beyond our simple understanding. Something that is felt but not known, we were there uninvited. By our own choice we had come, now we had to endure. "Mount your courage," I told Fish just as we heard the cracking of a palm tree. Whipped to a bow beyond its limit, the trunk broke with a thud. Still unable to see, the quiver of earth under our feet told us it was not nearby.

"In my courage I shall remain," said Fish. Nothing was to leave or enter this realm without permission, which we had been granted by not being flung into the sea.

Faintly a beam of sunlight found its way through a small translucent cloud, which hovered above the water. It was peculiar in the midst of grayness that was surrounding us. In the roaring sounds we had become drenched, our eyes still burning, but there not far down the beach near the patch of light we could see someone else.

A young man, his skin had the dark brown color achieved from spending a life outside in the hot sun. Muscles adorned his long lean limbs. Upon his head a mass of black hair blowing like loose feathers. Kneeling down with outstretched arms his fingers touching each gust as they became acquainted. Circling wind embraced him; in agreement he went with the wind gust. Silently without a splash or kick his body disappeared into the depths of the ocean. He was swept under by the currents and followed out to sea by the wind as it left us standing, unable to speak, not believing what we had just seen. The air was clear now and we could find our way to leave.

Pleasant warmth of a dry porch beckoned us home. When we arrived, exhaustion crept into every fiber. The minute we felt safe we slept through the night. The next day, birds woke us early, tweeting and whistling signals to one another. Nesting repairs were underway, requiring new territory to be established. Lucky for them there was a lot of building materials scattered about from the storm. The lake covering our park had shrunk on the outer edges, enough to expose earthworms trying to find a dry place.

Fish and I did not want to venture out onto the beach that next day, but we did want to take a look. Bracing my front paws against the rock wall, I extended my neck and head well above for a good view. Fish jumped up to sit on the flat landing atop and we both were looking for the same thing. Our heads facing the direction where we had heard the thud of a falling tree the day before. We had been thinking that possibly we both had the same dream. But there it was in plain sight, it had happened after all. The tree trunk laid across the sand with the green leaves swishing back and forth as the waves came in and out. Relieved that we had survived, our eyes scanned for what we knew was not there, the young man. Maybe he had been a vision. Debris cluttered the shoreline, waves lapped lazily under a bright yellow sun that opened the sky. A thin woman carrying a basket full of wood on her head strolled passed us slowly, tired from a long morning of gathering.

A week later to the exact day, we heard a commotion. Running through the muddy park we arrived at our gate where we saw a crowd of fishermen. They had found the body of a young man washed ashore at the same spot where we had seen him kneeling. No one knew who he was or where he had come from, but one thing was certain. Fish and I knew where he had gone after his misfortune of getting lost in a storm. He is now the Young Gust. Often we have wondered, had the gust of wind gathered to meet with him or had he gone there to be with the wind. I have brushed by a gust of wind and it recognized me. It was Young Gust and he is still strong.

At night when the moon is hidden we can see the wind swirling down our beach. In the fog it looks as if each gust of wind is dressed in an old uniform. They march as a company of soldiers, always with Old Gust leading. Young Gust is there too, his hair is still wild like loose feathers. Sometimes there are horses in the air, with the wind riding on their back. Against the ocean's grayness they disappear into the miles of sky just as we witnessed on a big rain day.

Life Will Go By In A Blink
Life Is As Quick As A Wink
If You Should Find Out Otherwise
This Would Be A Grand Surprise

I Know What Life Is To Me
I Take It So Sweetly
If You Wonder How I Know
It Is The Love For Me You Show

In Each Moment Is A Day
To Be Gone Is A Breath Away
If You Think It Is Forever
You Are Not Being Very Clever

Live Each Second In Your Love
Live In Peace From Above
If You Believe This Is True
Then My Friend I Will Be Seeing You

I AM WAITING

I am waiting, not sure what for, just waiting. Actually I am not waiting for anything particular, not for anything at all. I am just waiting here in the middle of the floor in front of the door. I am sitting and waiting, maybe the door is going to open. Often I use my intuition in situations like this, not sure what I will do next or which way to go when the door comes open. It's not that I feel I want the door to open or not to open. I just know it will and I am waiting. Footsteps are near, it is Laura, and she opens the door. I don't have to decide where to go or what to do, she picks me up, and we wiggle our nose to nose. Hello Precious, I hear her say, we go walk about to see Thomas. He is pasting pictures of trees and sea on paper. I really don't know why he does this when his garden is just outside, full of trees and sea nearby, but there he is with tape and paste and scissors and piles of pictures. He has a good collection of tree pictures and the sun over the sea. Carefully each is placed on a large paper. Many big pieces of paper, then each big paper is folded. He tells me they will be sent to people around the world. People who want to see what Bali looks like. If they like what they see we will have visitors, coming to hear the waves of our ocean, tasting the salty sea air as it fills each breath, walking with barefoot toes touching the sand. We wait for our visitor friends; our ocean waits, our trees wait, I am waiting. All will be the same for me when they come, I will hear them say Hello Precious. Hello precious ocean, hello precious trees, I am precious, we are precious. I like waiting not knowing whom for, just waiting.

FISH DINNER

I Will Give You Fish Tonight I Hope You Find
This To Your Delight
I Thought I Heard You Say, Just The Other Day
I Would Like Some Fish That Would Be My Wish
So It Is For You, Your Wish Will Come True
Pretty Kitty Cat What Do You Think Of That

Boiled Fish For You And Me Makes Us Both
Happy
On A Night Like This To Fill Your Tummy With
Warm Bliss
In The Rain There Is No Heat So Stay Inside With
Me To Eat
Dinner Time Is Near I Am So Glad You Are Here
Sweet Kitty Cat Beside Me You Have Sat

A Fish Of Your Own You Will Not Find A Bone

Prepared Just To Suit Your Taste Not A Crumb To Go To Waste

For You The Biggest Fish It Barely Fits On Your Dish

How Did You Eat It All When You Are So Small

Pretty Kitty Cat, Round You Are But Not Fat

A Fish Dinner We Did Share Now Sit With Me In My Easy Chair

Together We Will Stay Until Tomorrow's Day

Close You're Sleepy Eyes I Will Give You A Surprise

Milk When The Sun Is Bright In The Morning Light

Gentle Kitty Cat Fast Asleep These Moments We Shall Keep

JINX
THE ULTIMATE PRAGMATIST

There was a dreamer that dreamt a dream of the dog he would own one day. The more he dreamt the more he saw, him and his dog in play. This is a story about that dog, the dog that came to be. From a dream the dreamer dreamt, that dog is me.

My master is the dreamer, he is much older than I. It is lucky for me he never gave up dreaming of me as his young pup. Before I came to live with him, before I knew my name, I needed someone I could trust, to know me for what I am. I am not a simple housedog to keep the master entertained with silly tricks or sloppy licks, guarding is my game. I would never bite for fun but I would knock you down if you should run. That is how I like to play, to practice chasing the bad away.

Now, I have two ears that point above my head, but when I was young they didn't stand, they formed an X instead. Jinx, my master said, could be my name, perfect it was for me. The word means to bring bad luck and I will if you try to hurt my family. For you see that is my purpose I have known it all along and my body is undeniably Gladiator strong. To act on a purpose makes me a pragmatist. I am ultimate because I will act regardless of consequence. My purpose has become my nature because I understand and accept it to be a promise between my soul and my body.

Whenever someone comes to my house it is my job to analyze any potential threat by staring into the person's eyes. Near my master I will stand and very seldom do they ever stare back. If they did, it would mean a challenge to attack. My face looks just serious enough to help them understand, I am the ultimate pragmatist the grand defender of a man.

My master the dreamer summoned perfection in me and deserves my loyalty. He is my grand champion taking care of me to the best of his ability. Let me tell you a secret that none could be more true, the best dream of all is the dream that is dreamt by two. So remember how it came to be for my best friend and me. When you need a dream, become one and you will find the same I guarantee. I am Jinx in form and virtue the ultimate pragmatist.

There Was A Dreamer That Dreamt A Dream Of
The Dog He Would Own One Day.
The More He Dreamt The More He Saw, Him And
His Dog In Play.
From A Dream The Dreamer Dreamt This Is The
Dog That Came To Be
Perfection Was Summoned In That Dream,
Perfection Was Summoned In Me.

Before I Came To Live With Him, Before I Knew
My Name
I Knew Him, He Was My Dream And I Was His
The Same.
Let Me Tell You A Secret That None Could Be
More True

The Best Dream Of All Is The Dream That Is
Dreamt By Two.

His Dream Filled The Wind And It Blew Away
From His Head
It Came To Me And Became My Dream Instead
I Dreamed For A Special Friend And The Wind
Came My Way
It Blew My Dream Back To Him That Was My
Lucky Day

This Went On For Years And Years, Dreaming Of
Me As His Young Pup
I Dreamt Of Him As My Friend And Neither Of
Us Ever Gave Up.
I Knew Him And He Knew Me, Before We Ever
Met.
The Dreamer Is My Master I Am What He
Dreamt.

Remember How It Came To Be For My Best Friend
And Me
When You Need A Dream Become One And You
Will Find The Same I Guarantee
It Doesn't Matter How Long It Takes It Is Truly
Worth The Wait
Even If It Is Twenty Years There Is No Such Thing
As To Late

Send It In The Wind That Is What The Wind Is
For
To Deliver Your Dream And Come Back For
More
And Yes I Would Do It Again
Come To Earth To Serve My Friend

JUST A PUPPY

You're just a little puppy, trying to find your way
In a great big doggie's world, learning day by day

Not in the sense of body mass nor in the sense of skill
It is in your mind, I notice you are a puppy still

Sometimes at night when the tide is high and it makes a thumping roar
You don't know what that sound is and you pace from window to door.

If you hear the distant cry of a doggy lost in fear
It is important to you to bark telling it you are near

Helping you to calm yourself when you are full of joy
Trying to make you stay when another picks up your toy

116

Such a big puppy other dogs run away
The sadness in your eyes when they won't play

Standing eye to eye with a child that took your ball
to keep as his own,
Gently you took it from his hand and swiftly
brought your ball home

You were proud of your success and then you
found out
Not taking a toy away is what manners are all about

Your legs are like steel pipes your chest a barrel of lead
You never feel the pain you play to win instead

Stepping on your master's foot he got broken toes
They did not swell up like the day your head broke
his nose

Learning not to taste what you smell when you are
told
But for that plate of cookies you become so bold

Chasing the cobra is fun and pawing the frog is too
That is until your master starts hollering at you

It is hard for you to understand how we can
share so much
Yet when there is chocolate you are not
allowed to touch

He is still learning is what you hear us say
Just a little puppy changing every day

JUST WANT TO PLAY
Jinx finds compassion

I just want to play is what I told the little dog that I found on the beach today. He snarled and growled tried to bite, then he ran away. I followed him and chased him down, wait I said I just want to play. We can jump for joy like a wave and splash and roll and foolishly behave. He would not play he would not explain, just leave me alone is all he would say. No harm I bring to you I said just look and with my tail I shook. His ugly face he turned this way and that, he didn't know where to go. I stood insisting that he stay so we could spend some time in play.

He lurched to bite, he snarled and said I don't care about you, I don't care about anything. Again he tried to bite and in my heart I felt a sting. My feelings were hurt by his rejection, now the game had changed, he needed to be taught that it would be up to me if he were allowed to leave whether he liked it or not. Feeling sad and a little mad that he could be so mean I stood my ground making a choice should I attack and fight with all my might when really I just want to play.

It is not my nature to start a fight, though I would never back down. My size is enough to determine a battle, it is a fact that I will always win. So why would that dog be foolish enough to try and pick on me? Searching for an answer in his eyes I realized this dog is in misery. His fur is thin with bright pink patches of skin, his head is lowered in shame. For my lack of compassion in his pathetic life, I accepted blame. It is not his fault how I feel, my feelings belong to me. Feeling hurt or angry only means it is time to start feeling compassionately. I ran a circle around him to signal he could leave, saying to him maybe another day, as he quickly trotted away. Then he stopped to look at me and I heard him say. If wants and desires could come true, it would be mine to be just like you. He went around the bend, I watched until he was gone, thinking about wants and desires. I would desire for him to have no more pain and as for wants there is only one I have today. I just want to play.

Your Feelings Are Hurt When You Fail To Find

The Compassion You Have Within Yourself

On My Feelings I Will Never Act They Are My
Compass Or Guiding Star
To Help Me Find My Way Whether I Am Near Or
Whether I Am Far
Looking For That Place In My Heart Where I Have
Chosen To Be
In Anger And Pain Still Seeking To Live A Life
Compassionately

Easy To Get Lost Said The Compass To The Star
Only If They Don't Know Where It Is They Are.

LAW OF THE JUNGLE
The Umbrella Man

This place in all its diversity, one law remains, that which speaks to all in the same voice. The voice of knowing that whatever you have, whatever you own is yours only as long as you can keep it. That is the law of the jungle.

The umbrella that we saw was made in many bright colors. Underneath it walked the shadow of a man holding it with a trembling hand. Fish ran to hide in the shrubs, she never allowed him to come near. Jinx could smell him from a distance far, it made our nostrils flare. We both snorted at the air rather than breathe it in. This man with the pretty umbrella also carried fear, to us that meant he was dangerous.

His feet stomped back and forth down the walkway past the shrubs where Fish lay. Her eyes were round and wide watching so cautiously. Jinx was standing nearby with a glaring beady eye ready to defend Little Miss Fish, his cat friend. The umbrella man continued to stomp without a change in pace, he took no notice of them but Fish saw the look on his face. His brow was lumpy with ridges, his eyes had the color of yellow, his yellow lips were moving and his breathing was quick and shallow. Through the puddles of water his bare feet would stomp at the mud, splashing it on his pant leg, landing with a thud. He didn't seem to care, his head had been shaved, and there was no hair. His steps were taken in haste shaking and swaying as if he had no time to waste.

We watched as he crossed our park down to the ocean gate, we hurried to the pond for a better view but we were too late. The umbrella lying outside his door was the only trace that he had already entered into his place. A thatched roofed hut covered in vines in the corner of our wall, where the green leafed plants grow tall. At one time the gardens had been splendid but now growing with weeds the flowers were hindered. The umbrella man liked it that way, if his hut could not be seen he felt safe to sleep all day. He woke with the setting sun, it would take all night for his work to be done. Fish had seen him walking around in the middle of the night. Sometimes he stood behind a tall palm tree keeping out of sight. Wearing a sword in a sheath he would climb to the roof to watch the land beneath.

We waited near the edge of our park but he did not come out and it was almost dark. We remembered his eyes of yellow and wondered if he had a terrible fright. You see he is the keeper of the law, without him outside it is unsafe at night. Simple to understand, there is nothing you can do if your items are stolen, they do not belong to you. The fear he holds within himself keeps the thieves away. We thought about how strange it was to see him in the light of day. He knew he had to come for duty or all of our things could be gone. Now we began to worry there must be something wrong.

We had to enter his hut to see if he was all right and when we did it was a ghastly sight. He lay on his back upon his bed, from his mouth came a yellow foam. Fish shrieked and wanted to run home. Before she could leave I grabbed his sleeve, pulling him out of his bed. He rolled and thumped onto the floor, waking with a dizzy head. Fish was scared, she jumped to run to the door, on the way she knocked over a chair upon it a small bottle that rolled across the floor. The umbrella man reached out, the bottle rolled into his trembling hand. A bottle of pills from a doctor for malaria, now we understand. After he took his medicine he seemed to be just fine. I tried to stare eye to eye but he looked away from mine. Cleaning his face he stood up strong, he wanted us to see. That he was quite capable of performing his duty.

We had always looked at him as the keeper of the law, but now, the Lawman of the Jungle that is what we saw. The jungle crept into this man taking his life was the plan. It is yours if you can keep it, life or things the same law will apply. The law of the jungle is the same for all, on this you can rely.

If It Hadn't Been For Us Bumping Him Out Of His Fit As We Did.
He Would Be In His Coffin, They Would Be Nailing Shut The Lid.

INTO THE KITCHEN

Fish and Jinx

I could not have made myself clearer. Jinx, I said, come over here. Look at these tracks at our door. But Jinx only lifted his ear, my voice he chose to ignore. I knew how to get him on his feet fast. I just had to quickly prance past. He can never resist chasing a cat. He's on his feet, well look at that. I will lead him into the kitchen where our good chef bakes those sweet rolls and fruit pies and thickly frosted cakes.

Just like I planned, here he comes after me. Taking long strides, starting to run, he is gaining speed swiftly. Under the table I must dash and out the other side. But the chef is standing where I must go and the space that is left is not very wide. Too late to change, I gave it a try. Brushing by his ankle I hear a startled cry. What was that our chef said and just as he turned his head, Jinx had appeared, he could not stop, his stop turned into a skid. He lowered himself just enough under the table he slid. The table is short, Jinx is tall. When he stood up it all took a fall. The rolling pin, flour, a dozen eggs, spoons, sugar, melted butter and a great big bowl full of our chef's favorite batter.

The chef's big bowl flew into the air where it turned upside down spilling into his hair. Crashing when it hit the floor. I jumped onto his shoulders trying to reach the door. The sweet sticky dough was covering up his face. He couldn't see Jinx who had bolted like he was in a race. The chef was now screaming with me on his back. He tripped over Jinx sending us all down with a crack. When they looked for me they could only see my small paws track. I had made my escape. Leaving Jinx behind to clean up the mistake.

Jinx stood by the chef licking his face, he enjoyed the taste. No sense in having all this good batter go to waste. But he hollered at Jinx, the chef was mad. Jinx felt so very bad. He was sorry and wanted the chef to know. So as he left he hung his head low.

The rest of the day I washed and groomed. Jinx, he went back to his nap. I saw him asleep and whispered in his ear, sorry, I didn't want it to happen like that. Then I remembered the tracks outside the door. I went to take a second look and realized they were my tracks the same as I had left on the kitchen floor.

RUN WITH THE WIND

Jinx took me for a walk, he put his leash in my hand. We went to the beach to play in the sand. On the way we had to pass through the park covered in grass, around the pond where the tall ferns grow. To the gate in the wall, where we felt the ocean wind blow. From that point I was at his command. He knows more about the beach than I can understand. Like who passed by, where they came and where they went. With no one in sight he can tell by scent. He tugs at his leash with all his might. I can't keep up, I must hold on tight.

We came to a place where we could rest on a fallen palm tree that had failed the test of the pounding surf that pulled the root loose from its turf. There we sat to catch our breath and have ourselves a talk, I explained to him we are not here to run, we have come to take a walk. He looked at me with his beady eyes, he knew exactly what I meant and then I decided to give him a surprise, the time to run would be well spent.

The beach was empty except for us two, safer it could not be. Together we went to the water's edge and there I let him free. In that moment I shall never forget how mesmerized I was. By the grace, the power, and the speed of foot as I witnessed his spirit rise. He soared so smooth as if with the wind. His run was more like a reach. He flew, he sailed in between his toes barely touched the beach. It took only a couple of laps and back to earth he came. I know now why he likes to run. I wish I could do the same.

Our walk home was very slow, side by side; we listened to the ocean's flow. He looked at me occasionally as if to say I can do what you want. But it wasn't him, it was me that needed to be taught. Sometimes in a nature there are things that we cannot see. Jinx was not running alone; it was his spirit running with his body.

Trillalad Trillalad Trillalad
His Paws Upon The Wet Sand Mud
No Marathon Could Compare
Nor Feathered Bird In The Air

For This Is Not A Race
Nor Soaring In Life's Embrace
See The Expression On His Face
Breathing In God's Grace

He Accepts He Knows His Body To Be
The Tool Used To Set His Spirit Free
Blessed Be The Creature In Stride
May His Nature Be Our Guide

TWILIGHT LAND
A PLACE OF IMPERFECT CLARITY

It was not a long time, she was gone yet the thought of her not here sharing our life anymore filled us with sorrow. Even though we said she would return, there were moments when the tears stung our eyes and those few moments of uncertainty felt eternal. We refused to accept her gone for good because the thought was just too painful. Believing her desire to return was as strong as our desire to have her home if only she could find her way.

Bumper and Fish were staying with Mumzy for a few days while Thomas and Laura went to Singapore. She had traveled half way across the round world and had settled into a new villa. All were having a wonderful time together mostly because Mumzy always made everything so pleasant. Her villa had a tall rock wall that enclosed beautiful gardens where they explored together daily. She had taken great care to make sure it was a perfect place for the three of them, picking out big soft pillows and placing them exactly where Fish liked to nap, even providing a wide running bench for Bumper and a place for him to rest on her desk while she wrote letters. Every effort they appreciated but especially they enjoyed being with Mumzy, for she had quiet habits that were mixed with generous smiles and laughter often using her gentle voice humming soft melodies.

It was in the late afternoon on one of these peaceful days together that Fish had gone into the garden to sit on the ledge on top of the rock wall. Listening to the wild canaries twit and tweet, another sound caught her attention. It was the distant whisper of a long forgotten language, only used by cats that live in the dense forest of the jungle. Since leaving the forest as a small kitten Fish had not heard this language that still to this day she used instead of meow. In hopes of finding some of these rare cats, she jumped off her perch to follow that whisper of meong meong that carried lightly in the wind, tantalizing her perked ears.

Intent on the direction, using her shoulders in a pronounced, steady pace down the brick pathway. Now no longer a whisper, for the sound had become stronger and stronger with each stride. Until there, at the edge of a clearing with the jungle advancing on the far side was the source. Kittens tumbling, kicking and gnawing one another in play under the glow of a late sun. Fish lay low in the underbrush, listening, it had been the same for her just as for these small ones, the first word learned, meong meong. Remembering her days of careless joy, as with all little ones living wild and free, these days are not to last long. For they will be on their own, soon learning to be fierce, practicing their ancient traditions of survival. In her excitement of renewed memories her tail began to twitch. This subtle activity must have alerted the momma cat who suddenly sprang out from the camouflaged shade with her back arched, mouth hissing a throaty meong of her own, to threaten any perceived danger. Immediately the kittens scattered, they had been taught well and in that instant they were all gone, hidden back into the surrounding jungle. These shy creatures were not to be followed, preferring to hide only to attack the unsuspecting by surprise. Fish would leave the area to return home, more aware of the way her life used to be before she found her treasured companions Bumper and Mumzy. Content with the gentleness they had brought into her life and missing them more than ever she sprinted homeward, eager to share her experience.

One stretched leap to the wall ledge and into the yard just as the sun submerged daylight beneath the earth's rim. What had happened while she was away could not be imagined, all the flowers were gone. The lawn was sparse from lack of water and care. She hadn't been out that long yet everything was different. To the villa doors she went, checking each, none were open. The window shutters were closed she began to scratch at each until one that had not been latched was found. Prying it enough to squeeze through she went inside. No Bumper, no Mumzy, no pillows, nor water dish.

There were chairs with no cushions, a bed with no mattress, no soap and no towels. Panic began to strike, running up the wide stairs to the open air day room she found the huge four post bed with no covers, no mosquito net.

Evening was dissolving her hopes with dark shadows crossing the dusty floors. Spider webs hung in every corner, nothing was as it should be. It was a place of imperfect clarity in a time of decline, this was twilight land. Fish felt her breath tighten as her ribs constricted in fear. She must find a suitable hiding place in order to become calm. The standup cabinets on the main floor, quickly back down the stairs only to find the cabinet front door was closed. Crawling in from the back and climbing up to one of the selves, inside she was safe. In the lonely darkness of an unknown confusion Fish cried silently. Were the playful kittens a wayward dream? Had she risked all that is important to her for the glimpse of a dream? Her Bumper, she would do anything for her Bumper and Mumzy, please find me.

Bumper and Mumzy were not going to give up. They had already begun searching when she did not come home as expected for their favorite meal. Pink salmon for her, steamed broccoli with carrots for Bumper and hot bread with sweet cookies for Mumzy. Something had to be dreadfully wrong to miss a meal like that. Both had reached the conclusion that Fish must have left the yard and gotten lost since the outside area of the new villa was an unfamiliar territory. It was determined that Bumper would listen for her from the villa while Mumzy would search on the path outside. Taking the flashlight to shine on every shrub and tree, calling her name, listening for an answer there was nothing. With a heavy heart Mumzy went home regretting to tell Bumper about her lack of success. She knew his spirits would fall into grief, he was such a sensitive little rabbit. They would both need to agree that there is always hope.

No one lived in the villa next door that looked exactly the same as all the others except that this one had not yet been finished, the yard not planted and only sparse furniture. Mumzy had walked around this villa calling, and Fish had heard but it came from every direction. In her confusion of not knowing which way to go Fish did not answer remaining in her hiding place. She looked through the crack where the hinges attached and seeing no one there, decided to go upstairs to the day room for a better view. Hearing no reply Mumzy had already gone home, Fish never saw her.

With the night came a chill in the air, filling both villas with despair. They were all hungry, the ones that had food were too sad to eat. The one who would have eaten had no food. They must find one another and soon. Fish gathered every ounce of fortitude she had and surrendered to the higher power of the universe in a prayer. "May my blessed ears be filled with the sounds I desire to hear."

Mumzy was sitting with Bumper in their upstairs dayroom, they were saying a prayer together for the angel of guidance. Bumper asked Mumzy if she would make a special request of the angel. Since all things are possible, would the angel please take from my lips the name of Fish, put that name into the ears of the one that most desires hearing it and bring the name back to me. Mumzy was impressed at how specific Bumper's prayer had been and gladly obliged. Once they spoke the name Fish, it floated away out across the night air as an echo straight into the darkness of the villa next door and back again as if establishing a trail of direction. Bumper looked at Mumzy in wide-eyed amazement Mumzy smiled, she believed in the power of prayer.

Fish's name did fill her ears, she was still in the upstairs day room of the empty villa directly across from where they were. Running to the ledge with a timid weak voice saying meong meong which Bumper with his extraordinary ears immediately recognized. Joyous relief erupted into jumping up and down all three calling at the same time. Soon they would be together, but first a thank you God for your divine angel of guidance.

Fish remained where she was, while Bumper and Mumzy went downstairs and outside to the wall. Fish saw where they were, she ran down the stairs, out the shuttered window, across the yard, jumping up onto her own ledge, walking along straight into the outstretched arms of Mumzy, thrilled that her ordeal was over as they were now all home. It was way past bed time, almost midnight, but they were not going to bed. There was a lot of catching up to do as well as a late diner of Salmon, broccoli, cookies and drinks of milk all around.

Twilight Land Is Any Place Where There Is Imperfect Clarity At A Time When You Feel As If Your Life Is In Decline. Usually Found Between Where You

Have Been And Where You Want To Be. Should You Enter, It May Be Impossible To Ever Leave Unless You Have Enough Fortitude To Surrender. That Is The Only Way Out, It Is Required That You Surrender To The Higher Power Of The Universe.

UNDER THE WEATHER

Gravity, the reality of earth beckons the heaviness beneath the clouds to fall upon us in a shroud of moist heat. The body literally melts from within making it feel sheer as liquid. In appearance, the form and shape of our movement is thin and slow, clinging to the air like a wet rag. This is earth land; we live and breathe here under the weather.

Lightning crossed the sky tonight, it was only one color, very bright. It lit up our park as I looked in amazement, I heard the heavens bark. Like a dog in the sky that sounds the same as I. Listen to my thunder, with thunder I speak. I am Jinx and nothing about me is meek. I have heard a similar sound before when skies were blue and clear. It was an airplane I chased named Garuda, my master had said it was not allowed to land here. I did my best, it flew away. I was very proud of myself that day. Now every time it comes near our land, I chase it away on command. There is thunder in me, I am lightning fast with strength and stamina I will meet any task.

Now I feel the raindrops, they come from above I see. They are falling everywhere, they have come to play with me. I catch all I can with my tongue until the droplets come together one by one. Then they downpour upon my head that is the game we play for fun. It cools us in the nighttime and the ocean near the edge of our park leaps for joy and applauds, thumping the sand in a rhythmic arc. The falling rain fills it to its brim and in this game it joins in. Then the park lights up and the heavens bark and it all starts over again.

I am part of the storm an important part of the team. When we play at night you are probably in bed so just let me be part of your dream. Know that my voice is thunder and that I have lightning speed. I fear not the storm, it comes to play with me. It is me you hear in every storm, a game that's been going on since before you were born. So have no fear, know Jinx is near. I am playing a game tonight not a game to win but just to play with all my might to be a storm friend. I will let you on my team though chosen you must be. If you leave your fear behind to come and play with me. You don't even need to come outside I will do that for you. Just close your eyes and believe that what I say is true. My voice is in the thunder. My speed is lightning fast. Dream of you and me in play until the storm has past.

WHERE THERE IS LIGHT
Fish is brave

Sleeping where there is light is the best sleeping for me. It is not that I am afraid of the dark, the fact is, the dark is afraid of me. I am a skilled hunter, which I cannot deny. I can listen to find what I cannot see. I can smell what I hear to tell me how near. I attack, I taste all without fear. In the dark I am wild. In the dark I am free. So if I want to sleep, I sleep where there is light and when I need to hunt I enter the night. All children seem to know this at some time in their life. Mostly when they grow older they forget what it is like. That is just the way it is for many others and me. That's the way it is for children and beast that believe. They believe to know what they have yet to learn. They have yet to learn what they already know. That the bravest of the brave who wants to sleep, sleeps where there is light.

My friend is a woman, her name is Laura. My name is Fish we live here with our dog named Jinx. He thinks he is so smart with his bark bark bark. I am not so sure he is as smart as he thinks, he sleeps soundly in the dark. I must not forget our family man Thomas. Neither Laura nor Thomas knew why it was that when they turn out the lights for bed, I would not stay in the house with them but go to the porch instead. Jinx was the first to find out. He wanted me to stay inside and play. I scratched his nose to remind him how really brave I am. He said he had forgot but never would again. I think he really had not forgot but just said that to get his way. But if he forgets I will do the same, I have been reminding him every day. Thomas, he knows I am brave, he has always been true to me. Sometimes I bring him a rat to brag, I am so proud to make him happy. It was Laura, after a very long time, seemed to know just recently the nature of my ways. I always spend each evening beside her in our chair. A chair just right for the two of us where not ever a dog would dare. We watch TV, she brushes me after I have had my milk. Then she whispers, you sleepy cat you are just as sweet as you can be. On this one night she learned what I needed her to know. I heard her say to

Thomas it is windy outside I don't want her to go. Fish couldn't be hunting every night, maybe she has been sleeping in the porch light. Of course I am, I wanted to say but they were gone. They had left the lights on and there in our chair I slept until the next day.

The hunter, the beast, the king of the jungle, the night watches over me. So if I want to sleep I sleep in the light. Where there is light it is heavenly.